Our Solar System

Jupiter

Neptune

Uranus

Io

Ganymede

Europa

Jupiter's Moons

Saturn

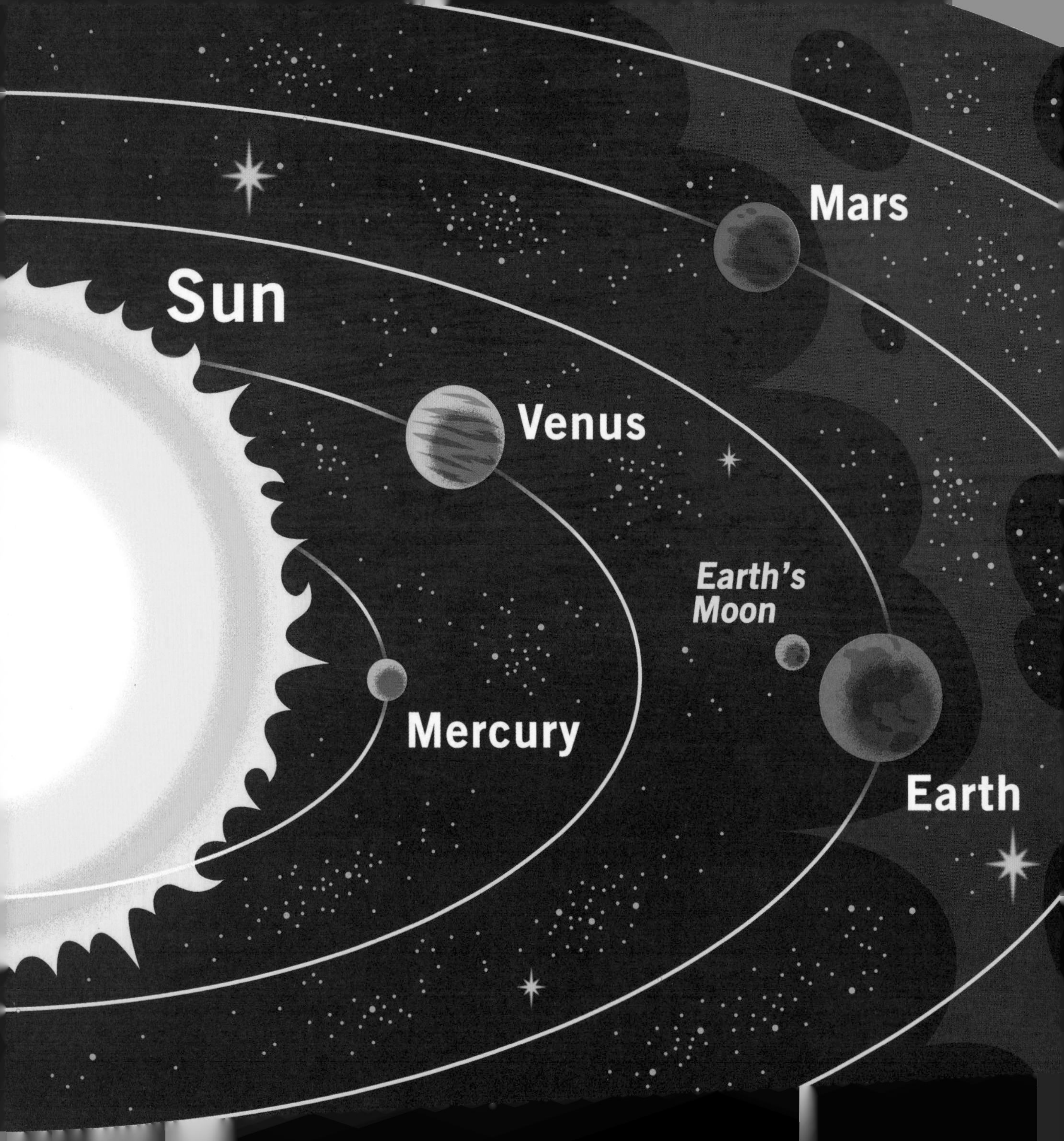
Sun
Mars
Venus
Earth's Moon
Mercury
Earth

A Gift For:
From:

Story time and play time are a lot more fun when You're The Star!

Story time

1. Put on the cape and secure it around your shoulders.
2. Turn the device to ON using the switch located on its side.
3. Press the front of the device one time to begin story time!

- *When an adult reads the highlighted phrases in the book, you'll hear music, voices, and other sounds.*

Play time

1. Put on the cape and secure it around your shoulders.
2. Turn the device to ON using the switch located on its side.
3. Press the front of the device two times to begin play time!

- *Say the trigger phrases listed in the back of each book to hear more sounds and to make play time even more fun!*

Collect all of Cosmic Ray's books to find out more magical phrases!

Published by Hallmark Gift Books,
a division of Hallmark Cards, Inc.,
Kansas City, MO 64141
Visit us on the Web at Hallmark.com.

Editorial Director: Carrie Bolin
Editor: Emily Osborn
Art Director: Jan Mastin
Designer: Scott Swanson
Production Designer: Dan Horton

ISBN: 978-1-59530-656-2
KOB8096

Printed and bound in China
OCT13

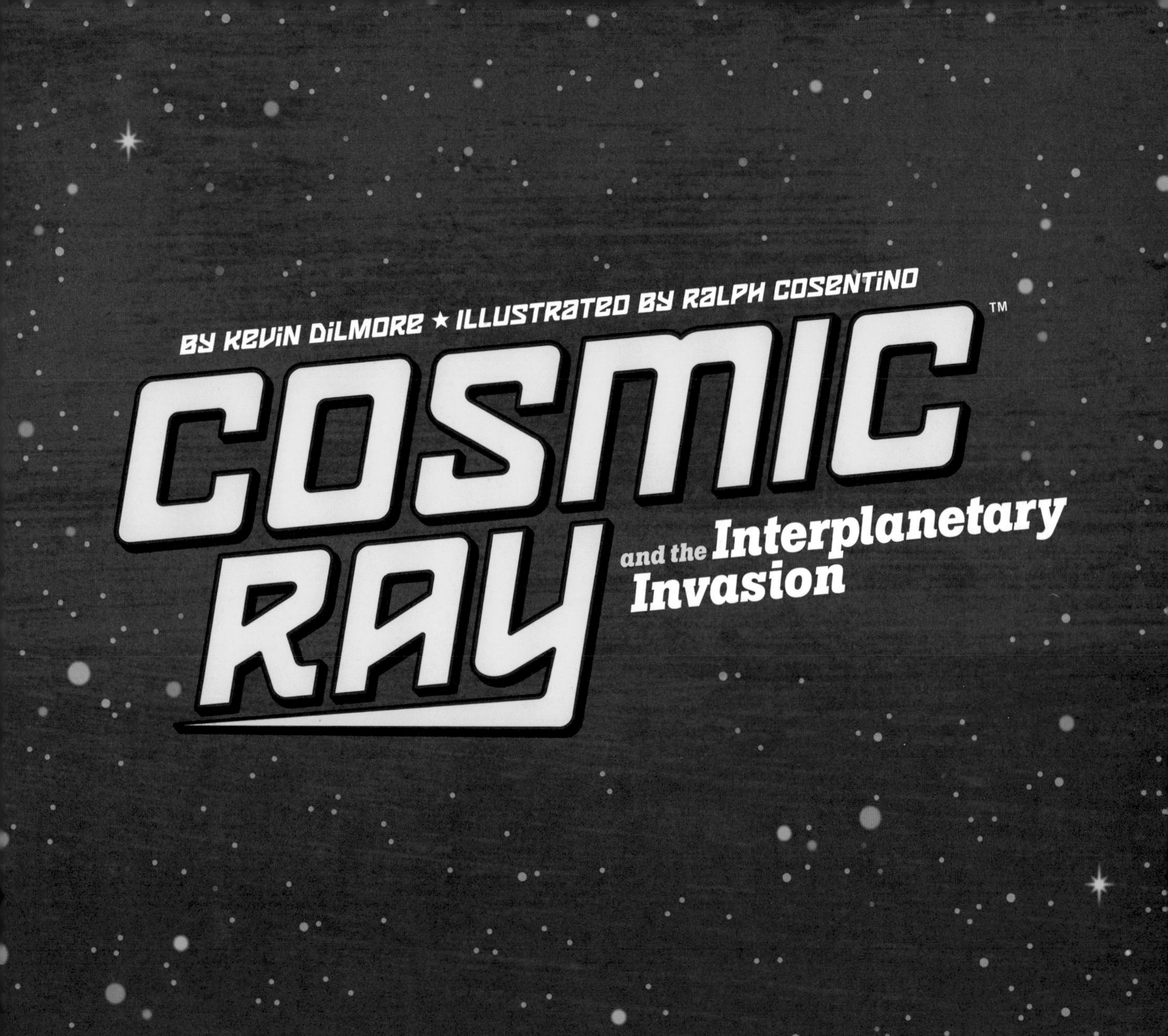
BY KEVIN DILMORE ★ ILLUSTRATED BY RALPH COSENTINO
COSMIC RAY™
and the Interplanetary Invasion

Hallmark

"Hey, Mr. Van Allen! Watch this!" Raymond held his hand up in the air. "Cosmic power, come to me!" From across his neighbor friend's yard, Raymond's alien device rose from the ground and flew into his grip.

“Wow, Raymond,” said Mr. Van Allen. “You’ve learned to control the device even when you’re not wearing it!”

“I’ve been practicing,” Raymond said. “I want to be the best hero I can be.”

Mr. Van Allen stroked his chin and said, “I’m glad you have been thinking about how this thing works.”

“We’ve unlocked some powers from the sun and moon,” Raymond said, “but I want to know what this means.” He pointed to a swirling design inside the device.

“That looks like a black hole,” said Mr. Van Allen. “Black holes are deep in space and have gravity so strong that nothing can escape them, not even light itself.”

“Whoa!” said Raymond. “That could be the strongest power the device has! I will have to be careful with that one.”

Meanwhile, the scientist Dr. Krankey tuned his deep-space viewer to communicate with an alien spacecraft that just arrived on Earth. "I am ready to help begin your invasion of the planet," he said through a fiendish smile, "and take over the world!"

"Excellent," the alien voice said. "A shuttle is coming to bring you to our ship. We will need the cosmic power device from you."

Dr. Krankey shook his fist. "I don't have it! I cannot get it from the boy!"
"If you cannot take it back," said the alien, "*we* will!"

Back at Mr. Van Allen's house, Raymond felt the ground start to shake under his feet. Suddenly, a beam of bright light struck Raymond and Mr. Van Allen, ripping a chunk of ground from the yard and pulling them into the air with it!

Raymond looked back to see how high they were already—higher than even an airplane. "They better hang on," he said, "because here comes Cosmic Ray!"

The beam set them down on the floor inside the ship. A metal door opened to reveal the alien invaders .

Mr. Van Allen whispered, “They don’t look happy.”

“I have an idea,” Cosmic Ray said. “This floor looks pretty slick.”

Cosmic Ray focused his imagination and shoved his arms hard out in front of him. The closest robot shook as if it had been pushed, then started to slip! It tipped into the other two robots and they all fell to the floor with a boom like thunder!

Then Cosmic Ray grabbed Mr. Van Allen and ran for the door at the speed of light!

Cosmic Ray turned to the metal doors. "I'll slow them down after I turn up the heat!" He crossed his wrist bands to focus his powers and melt the doors together.

"Quick! This way," said Mr. Van Allen as they ran down the hallway and through another set of metal doors.

"Aha!" said Dr. Krankey. "Now we've got them!"

The alien leader stepped forward. "We will take the device now, Cosmic Ray."

"Indeed!" Dr. Krankey shrieked. "I'll need it to take over the world!"

The alien leader laughed and pointed at Dr. Krankey. "Not so fast," he said. "We decided it would be easier not to *rule* your world, but to *destroy* it!"

"What's in it for me then?" asked Dr. Krankey.

The alien leader leaned in closely to Dr. Krankey. "We will let you live."
"That's it? You're crazy!" Dr. Krankey looked at Cosmic Ray. "Well, stop them!"
"Come on!" Cosmic Ray grabbed Mr. Van Allen and ran at the speed of light.

Cosmic Ray knew just what to do. "Can you fly this?" he asked Mr. Van Allen. Mr. Van Allen nodded. "We can figure it out."

Dr. Krankey ran to a shuttle of his own, yelling, "I'm getting out of here!" And then the two shuttles shot into space.

Cosmic Ray ran to the shuttle hatch, took off his cosmic power device and quickly threw it out into open space.

"Wait!" Mr. Van Allen shouted. "What are you thinking?"

"Trust me. It's the only way," said Raymond, looking like his normal self again.

"I have to focus and imagine," he said, "to create a black hole!"

Instantly, the huge spaceship got sucked into the device's mysterious black hole and completely disappeared!

Back on Earth, Raymond and Mr. Van Allen watched the night sky. "What do you think happened to Dr. Krankey?" Raymond asked.

"It's impossible to say for sure, but I imagine we haven't seen the last of him," Mr. Van Allen said. "You did a very heroic thing up there, Raymond. You gave up the device to save the Earth."

"Oh yeah?" Raymond held his hand up in the air. "Cosmic power, come to me!" Something was flying through the sky. The device sailed right into Raymond's hand. "See, I told you I've been practicing!"

Turn the page
for even more
fun with COSMIC
RAY

Press the device one more time, then try saying these phrases when you're out playing!

I gotta fly!
I'll save you!
It's hero time!
Now you see me, now you don't!
Take that!
Ready, set, go!
Let's do this!

NEW

Fire it up!
Look out!

Discover even more fun phrases in other Cosmic Ray books!

If you have enjoyed this book or it has touched your life in some way, we would love to hear from you.

Please send your comments to:
Hallmark Book Feedback
P.O. Box 419034
Mail Drop 100
Kansas City, MO 64141

Or e-mail us at:
booknotes@hallmark.com

Our Solar System

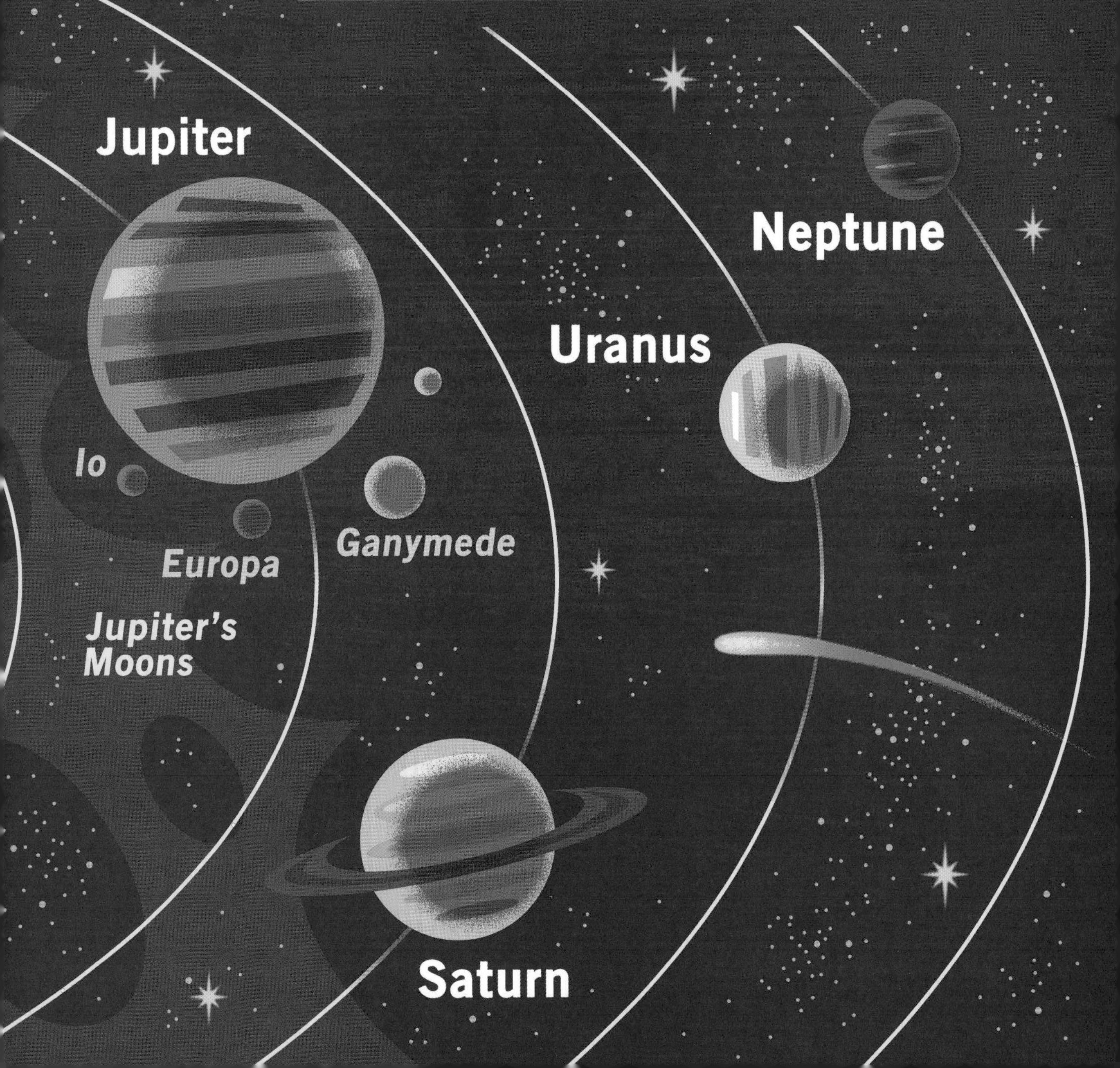

Jupiter

Neptune

Uranus

Io

Ganymede

Europa

Jupiter's Moons

Saturn

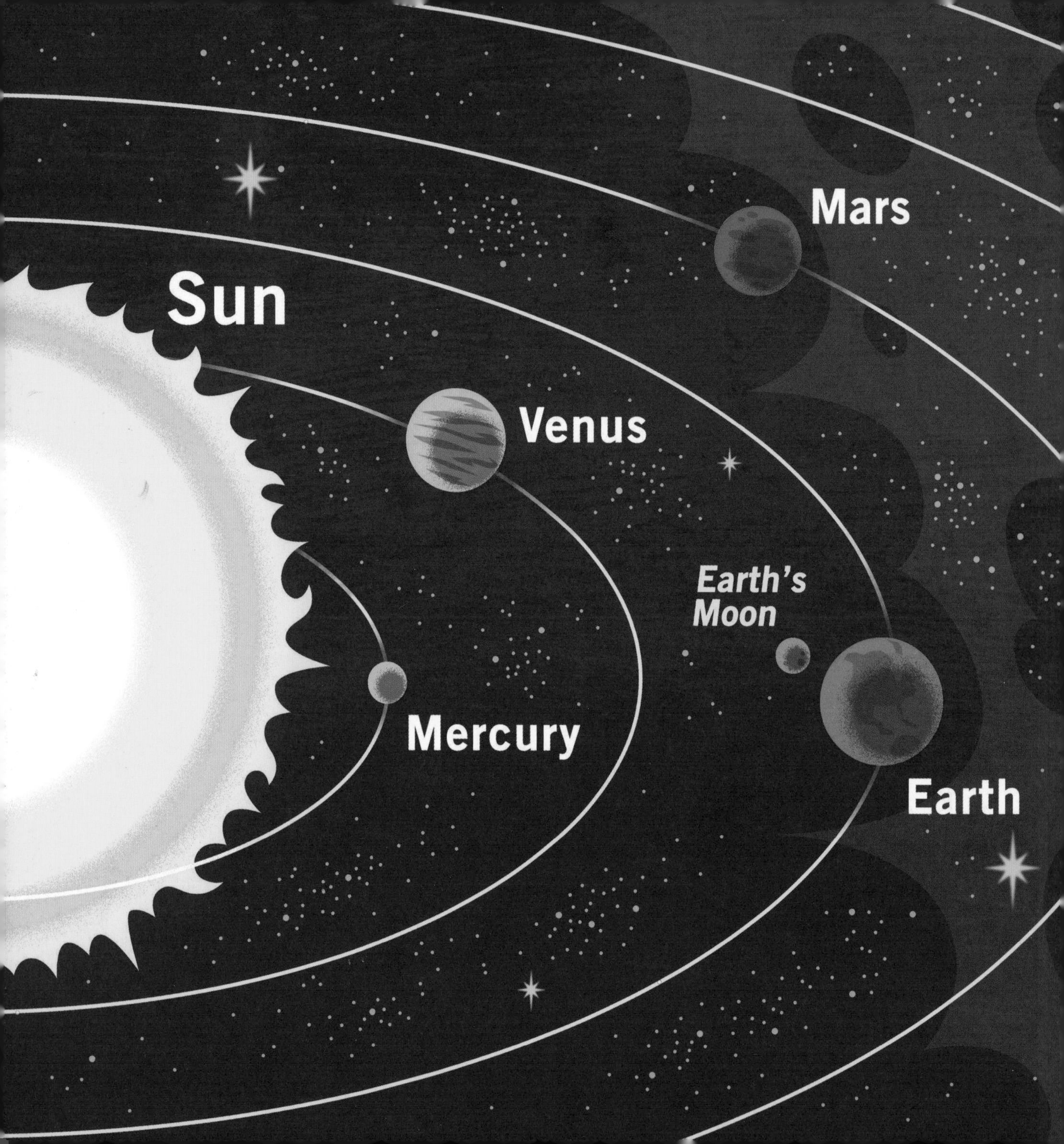
Mars
Sun
Venus
Earth's
Moon
Mercury
Earth